My Preschool

My Preschool

ANNE ROCKWELL

Henry Holt and Company

New York

There are lots of places I go
that are away from home.
But my favorite is preschool.

This is my preschool.

My cubby is right inside the door.

It's where I put my backpack and vest.

Miss Andrews and
Mrs. Dominic are always
there to say good morning.

Marcus   Mary   Will

I don't know why Melissa cries every time she says good-bye to her mother. I don't. I love to come to preschool.

I think Melissa does, too. I think she isn't really sad because she always stops crying as soon as we go to the water table to play.

"Splish, splash! Splish, splash!"
This is the song Melissa sings as she
makes the whale dip and dive.

I try to hold the water in my hands and
watch it make a waterfall as it flows out.

When everyone arrives, it's circle time.
We say good morning to our teachers and friends.
Some of us have special stories to tell.

We raise our hand if we do.

I tell about how a raccoon tipped over

our garbage can last night.

"What a mess!" Daddy said.

At play time Steve and I make the trucks go "Vrooom! Vrooom!" across the sand table.
Then Mr. Bill arrives.

Mr. Bill is our music teacher. He tunes
his guitar and we sing "Old MacDonald."
Or sometimes we sing another song.

Yoga time is when we stretch
and pretend we're something else.

My favorite pose is the cat.

Emma likes to be the cobra.

Marcus likes to be a tree.

When it's time for our snack,
I sometimes get to pass out the
paper cups.
But today it's Mary's turn.

When we were building with blocks, Will got mad and knocked all my blocks down.

I don't know why.

Miss Andrews had a private talk with him, and he said he was sorry.

We played together outside,
and Will wasn't mad at me anymore.

This is the smock I put on when it's time for art.

I stick my brush in the bright and gooey paint, and spread it across the paper on the easel.

Look at the painting I'm making!

Mommy will love this one.

She loves all the paintings I make.

We sit in a circle on the rug again when it's story time. We listen and look and keep quiet until the story is over.

This story is good. I wish Mrs. Dominic would read it all over again.

"Another day," she says, when I ask her.

There are so many things to do at my preschool, I never want to go home.

But there is Mommy!

Guess what!

When Mrs. Dominic and Miss Andrews say good-bye at the door, Melissa starts crying because she doesn't want to go home.

But I do . . . because I know I will come to preschool again tomorrow.

For Francis, Vincent, and Elena

With thanks to Julianna Brion
for her help in printing the monotype art.

Henry Holt and Company, LLC
Publishers since 1866
175 Fifth Avenue
New York, New York 10010
www.HenryHoltKids.com

Library of Congress Cataloging-in-Publication Data
Rockwell, Anne F.
My preschool / Anne Rockwell.—1st ed.
p.   cm.
Summary: Follows a little boy during his day at preschool, from cheerful hellos in circle time,
to painting colorful pictures and playing at the water table, to passing out paper cups for snack.
ISBN 978-0-8050-7955-5
[1. Nursery schools—Fiction. 2. Schools—Fiction.] I. Title. II. Title: My pre-school.
PZ7.R5943Myh 2008   [E]—dc22   2007002834

First Edition—2008 / Designed by Laurent Linn
Printed in October 2009 in China by Midas Printing Group Ltd.,
Dongguan City, Guangdong Province, on acid-free paper. ∞

5 7 9 10 8 6 4

The artwork is hand-printed monoprint using a traditional Japanese *baren* instead of
a press-on handmade Japanese Ise Washi paper. The inks are Akua-Kolor nontoxic inks.